P9-BBS-817

Text by Calliope Glass

Illustrated by Andrew Phillipson, Scott Tilley,
and the Disney Storybook Artists

Designed by Stuart Smith

Copyright © 2010 Disney Enterprises, Inc./Pixar. Disney/Pixar elements © Disney•Pixar, not including
underlying vehicles owned by third parties; Hudson Hornet is a trademark of Chrysler, LLC; Fiat is a
trademark of Fiat S.p.A.; Porsche is a trademark of Porsche; Mercury is a registered trademark of Ford
Motor Company; Jeep® and the Jeep® grille design are registered trademarks of Chrysler LLC; Model T
is a registered trademark of Ford Motor Company; Sarge's rank insignia design used with the approval
of the U.S. Army; Chevrolet Impala is a trademark of General Motors; Mack is a registered trademark
of Mack Trucks, Inc.; Dodge is a trademark of Chrysler LLC; Mazda Miata is a registered trademark
of Mazda Motor Corporation; Ferrari elements are trademarks of Ferrari S.p.A.; Monte Carlo is a
trademark of General Motors; Darrell Waltrip marks used by permission of Darrell Waltrip Motor
Sports; Cadillac Coupe DeVille is a trademark of General Motors; Volkswagen trademarks, design
patents and copyrights are used with the approval of the owner Volkswagen AG.
All rights reserved. Published by Disney Press, an imprint of Disney Book Group. No part of this book
may be reproduced or transmitted in any form or by any means, electronic or mechanical, including
photocopying, recording, or by any information storage and retrieval system, without written
permission from the publisher. For information address Disney Press, 114 Fifth Avenue,
New York, New York 10011-5690.

Printed in the United States of America

First Edition

10 9 8 7 6 5 4 3 2 1

G942-9090-6-10274

Library of Congress Catalog Card number on file.

ISBN 978-1-4231-3154-0

Visit disneybooks.com

For Text Pages Only

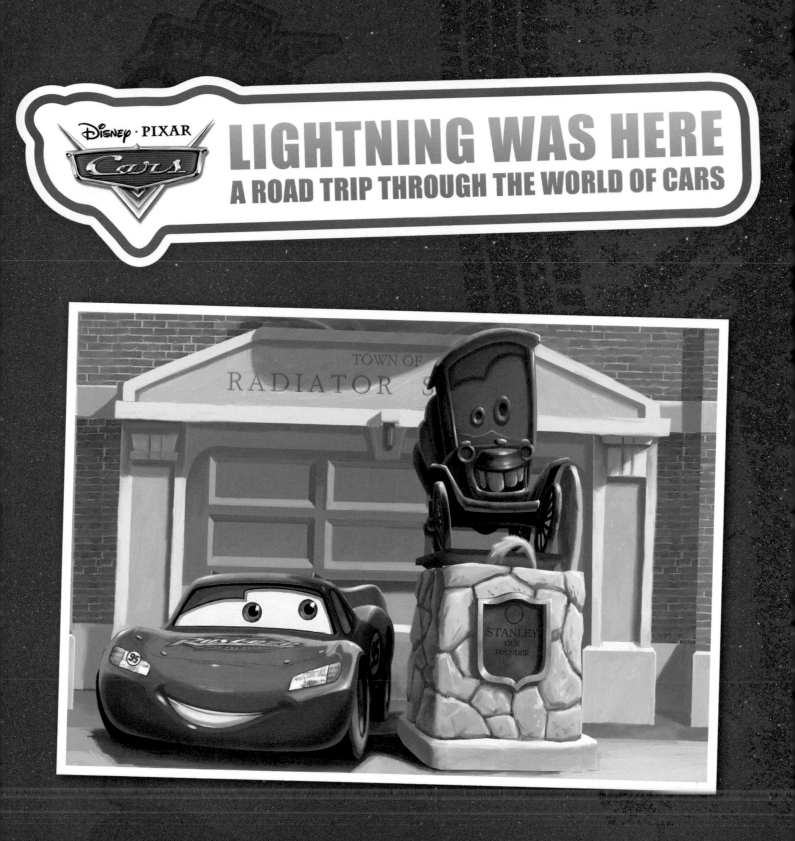

Disney · PIXAR
Cars

LIGHTNING WAS HERE
A ROAD TRIP THROUGH THE WORLD OF CARS

Disney PRESS
NEW YORK

Hello! I'm Lightning McQueen. Back when I started racing, I was a fast rookie race car with big dreams. I didn't care about anything except the next race; I didn't even care about having a place to call home. Home wasn't important—all that mattered was winning.

But then, on my way to the biggest race of my life, I found myself in the sleepy little town of Radiator Springs. At first, I tried to get out of there. But pretty soon the cars there became my friends—and Radiator Springs became my home. And let me tell you, it's a home worth seeing! So come along, and I'll show you around—with a few side trips along the way.

MOTOR SPEEDWAY OF THE SOUTH

Our first stop is where it all began—a racetrack, of course! This arena was where I got my big break. I had no way of knowing that the Dinoco 400 race would end in a tie and start me on my way to Radiator Springs. All I knew was that I was determined to win the race—and the Piston Cup.

News helicopter

Souvenir-sales car

News crews on the roof

Crowds of spectators

Lightyear blimp

RSN SKYBOX

TV screen

Darrell Cartrip

RSN RACING SPORTS NETWORK

RSN RACING SPORTS NETWORK

htB

Bob Cutlass

Microphones

Sweet paint job!

The Racing Sports Network skybox is where the commentary on the race happens. Those announcers can be pretty funny!

PIT CREWS

Forklifts

DINOCO

The pit crews keep the races going—changing tires, gassing up the race cars, and making sure nothing breaks down.

This is where the die-hard fans get together. I love these guys! They bring the fun to every race.

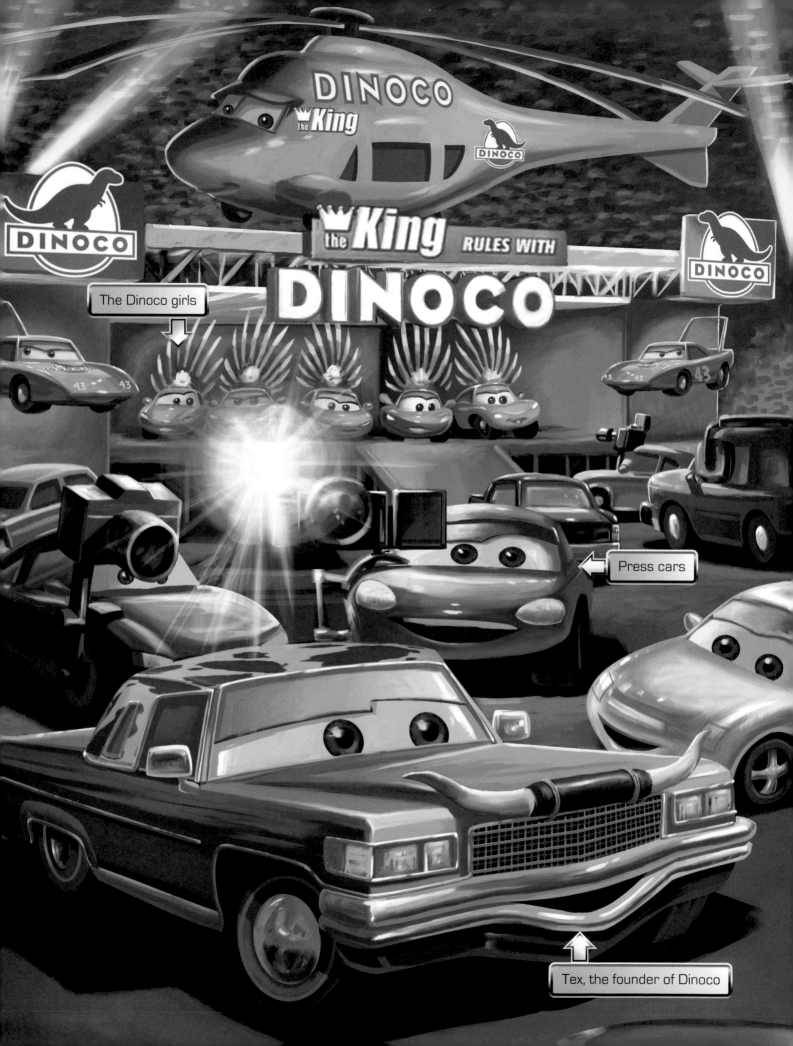

The Dinoco girls

Press cars

Tex, the founder of Dinoco

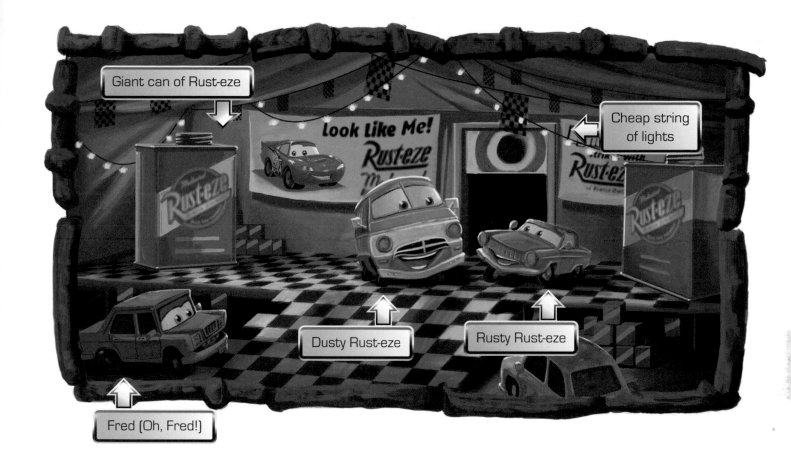

Giant can of Rust-eze

Cheap string of lights

Dusty Rust-eze

Rusty Rust-eze

Fred (Oh, Fred!)

Every race car dreams of being sponsored by Dinoco. They're the glitziest, the coolest, the best!

And then there's Rust-eze, my sponsor. You can see from the inside of their tent that they're not exactly glitzy, but these guys have hearts of gold. And that's what counts.

MACK'S TRAILER

Back in those days, Mack's trailer was the closest thing I had to a home.

Rust-eze logo

Back end lowers into a ramp

Lightning McQueen 95

Big picture of yours truly! (Ka-CHOW!)

Yet another Rust-eze logo

Check out all the cool things inside! I spent many a night in this fancy trailer, dreaming of winning the Piston Cup. But these days, when I'm on the road, I'm usually thinking about Radiator Springs.

Toys, stickers, dolls (All me!)

Plaques and trophies (All mine!)

Stereo

Mood lighting!

"Stars" on the roof

Mack on video

Personal car wash

Simulated windows

Radiator Springs

Here we are at last—the place I call home! I'll never forget the night I tumbled out of Mack's trailer and into this little town. From Flo's V8 Café to Mater's tow yard, you can tell Radiator Springs has personality. It's true that when I first arrived here, I couldn't wait to leave. But then I started to appreciate its charms, one by one. . . .

Cozy Cone

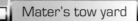

Mater's tow yard

Casa Della Tires

The Courthouse

Ramone's House of Body Art

Radiator Springs Curios

Flo's V8 Café

Sarge's Surplus Hut

Fillmore's dome

IMPOUND LOT

I spent my first night in Radiator Springs locked up in here.
Not much of a welcome! But I sort of had it coming.

Rusty old
oil drums

Rusty old barbed wire

Rusty old fence

RADIATOR SPRINGS COURTHOUSE

This was my second stop in Radiator Springs. Take it from me—traffic court is no fun, especially when you're guilty of tearing up an entire stretch of road.

This little fountain represents the freshwater spring Stanley found here—the reason he decided to settle in this area.

Red the fire truck →

Statue of Stanley, the founder of Radiator Springs

At least the courthouse is interesting, both outside and inside.

Doc is the town judge.

Lizzie

Portrait of Stanley

Highway guardrails

Sheriff

Sally is the town attorney.

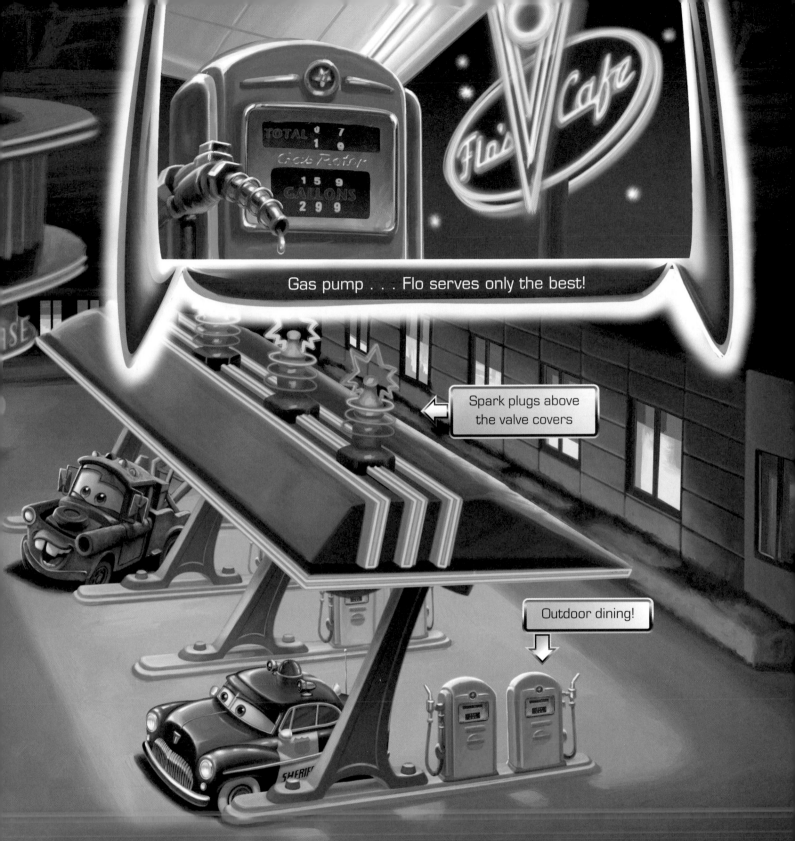

Gas pump . . . Flo serves only the best!

Spark plugs above the valve covers

Outdoor dining!

FLO'S V8 CAFÉ

The courthouse is nice to look at, but traffic court just isn't my scene.
I prefer Flo's V8 Café! When I arrived in town, Flo was very nice to me.
I couldn't believe I had to repave Main Street instead of getting my tailpipe
out to California for the tiebreaking Dinoco 400 race!

The inside of Flo's is awesome—you can get all sorts of treats here. Gas, antifreeze, coolant, axle grease . . . Flo even has a Sludgee machine. And there are jukeboxes at the counter! Mater loves listening to his favorite song, "Boundin'."

Glamour shots of Flo from her Motorama Girls days →

← Gas counter

Mater →

Flo's is cheery enough during the day, but at night, when Flo turns on the neon—*Ka-CHOW!*

Ramone installed this chandelier for Flo. He used his hydraulics to get up high enough to reach the ceiling!

Jukebox

Sally

Ramone's House of Body Art

Flo and Ramone met way back when, and they've been together ever since. You go to Flo's when your tank is empty, and you go to Ramone's when your paint job is boring. He'll brighten you right up!

Check out these cool hoods!

Sample paint styles

Ramone and Flo live here.

My new paint job!

MATER'S TOW YARD

Mater is my best friend in Radiator Springs. He's got a heart the size of a semi, and he isn't afraid to backfire in public. I've learned a lot from Mater. He taught me how important it is to have friends and a place you can call home. (He also taught me the finer points of tractor-tipping and driving backward.) The tow yard is Mater's pride and joy.

Crooked shack

Mater!

Give him a call if you find his hood!

CASA DELLA TIRES

Luigi runs a spiffy tire shop here in Radiator Springs. He very kindly lets me buy tires from him (even though I'm not a Ferrari).

Guido's "leaning tower of tires"

String lights (like in the Rust-eze tent!)

Luigi's

CASA DELLA TIRES

Spare tires

Luigi

Red the fire truck likes to water the plants at Luigi's.

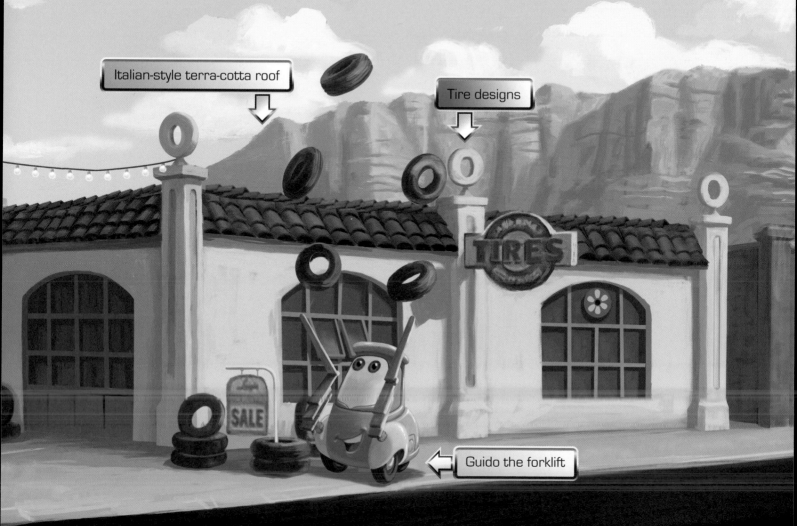

Italian-style terra-cotta roof

Tire designs

Guido the forklift

Here's where the magic happens! These two make a great team. Luigi's taste and Guido's skill keep everyone rolling in style.

Luigi's highest quality whitewall, "Fettuccini Alfredo"

Ferrari posters

Mirrors for modeling new tires

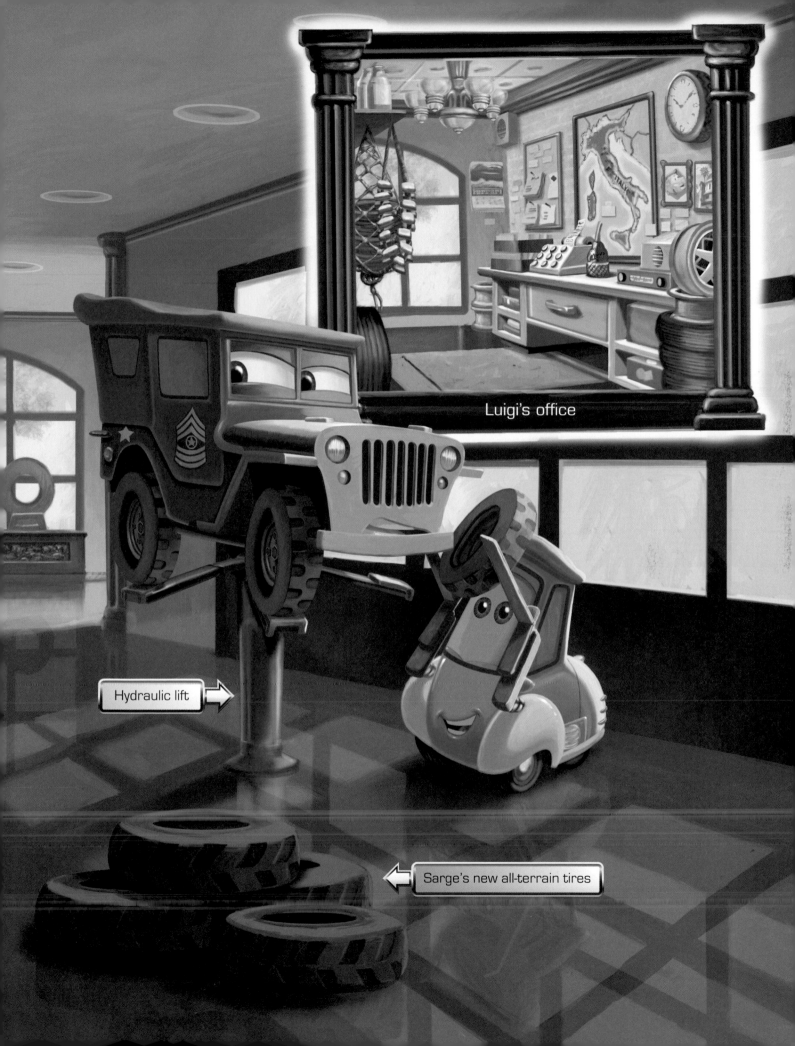

Luigi's office

Hydraulic lift

Sarge's new all-terrain tires

Rooms ⟹

Patio umbrellas ⟸

THE COZY CONE MOTEL

I spent my first night in Radiator Springs at the impound lot. But my second night was a lot nicer—I stayed at the Cozy Cone! It's quite a place. Sally's the owner, and her hospitality can't be beat—and if you like traffic cones, you'll love this hotel! If you don't like traffic cones, well . . . good luck getting a good night's sleep.

Sally runs a tight ship—I mean, cone.
The office is where she meets any guests
who come to stay at the Cozy Cone.

Cone-shaped
cactus pots

Desk fan

Cone lamp

Desk bumper

Room 1, where I stayed!

Cone lighting

Cone-shaped pictures of cone-shaped buildings!

Cone wallpaper

Cone alarm clock

Curb cones

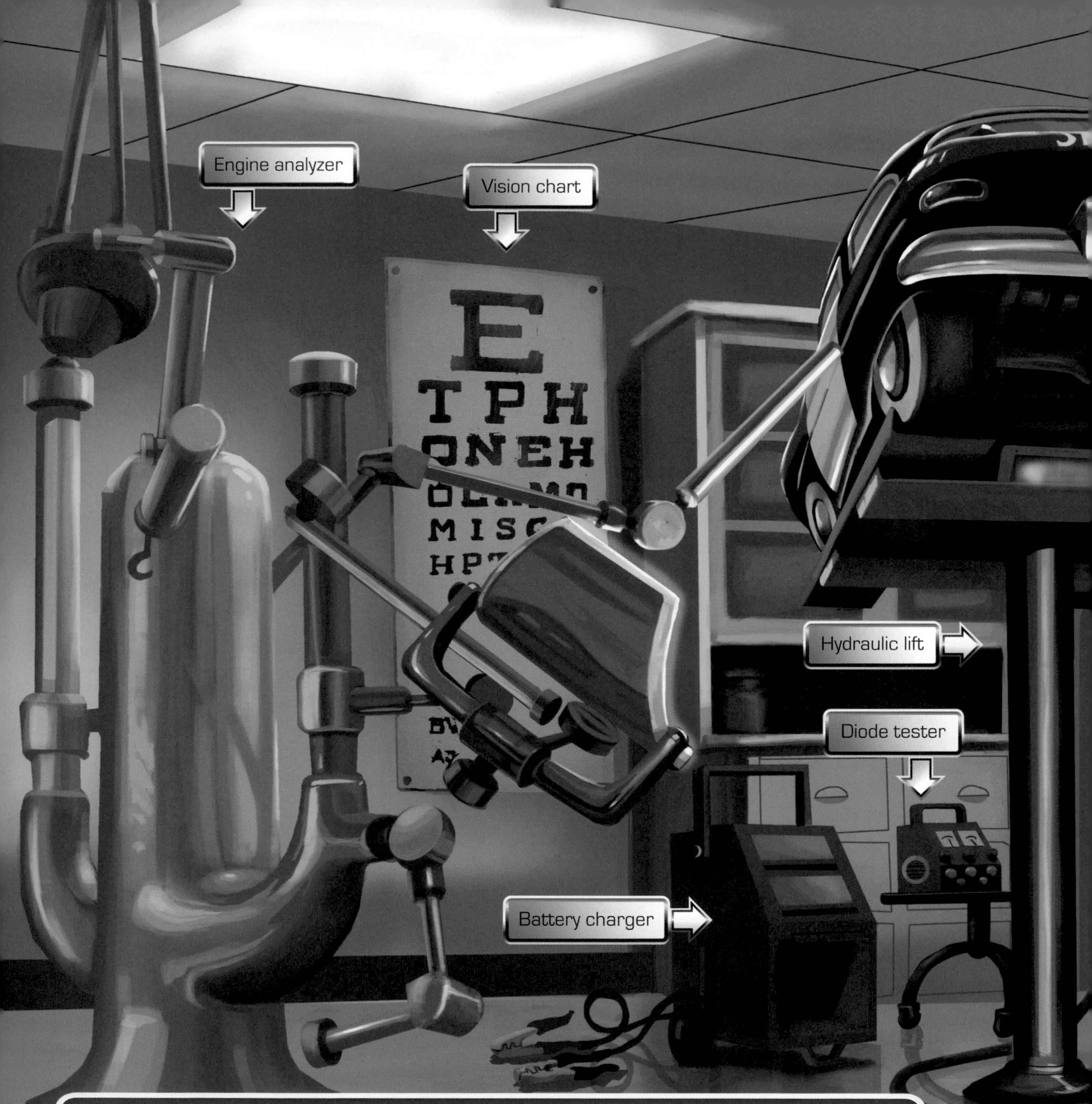
Engine analyzer
Vision chart
E
T P H
O N E H
Hydraulic lift
Diode tester
Battery charger

DOC'S MECHANIC CLINIC

Doc is one impressive car. He's the town judge *and* the town doctor! I've got tons of respect for him. But we didn't always get along so well. In fact, when I first arrived in Radiator Springs, Doc didn't like me, and I didn't like him. But eventually we found some common ground. . . .

The outside of Doc's clinic. Nice, huh?

Surgical lights

X-ray machine

Wrenches (ouch!)

Tach/dwell tester

Armature tester

Oil pan

Old newspaper clippings

CRASH! HUDSON HORNET OUT FOR SEASON

Old belts

Old papers

Old boxes

DOC'S GARAGE

Not long after I arrived in Radiator Springs, I discovered that Doc had a secret past—he used to be a race car like me! And not just any race car, either. Doc was the Hudson Hornet. He won the Piston Cup. In fact, he won three Piston Cups!

RADIATOR SPRINGS CURIOS

Oh, boy! What can I say about Lizzie's shop? Well, you can read the signs for yourself: U WANT IT WE GOT IT. And also: JUNK. Lizzie is one of a kind, all right.

Antique signs

Antique
gas pumps

Lizzie was married to Stanley,
the town's founder!

Lizzie's specialty is bumper stickers. She can't resist decorating anyone who comes in! Lizzie's definitely a classic—no matter how much Radiator Springs may change, she never will.

Posters

Antique road signs

Antique license plates

Snow globes

Collectible hubcaps

35YBL SBK656 TNK702 46457 BI324CA FBU567

RADIATOR SPRINGS CURIOS

Just like the real thing!

32789 GK224 11AB17 45398 BI324CA SBK656

NICE BUTTE!

I Auto be in Pictures

you Tailgate, I BACKFIRE

Lizzie's favorite bumper stickers

Bumper stickers

Souvenirs

THE WHEEL WELL

The Wheel Well is a hotel from the boom days of Radiator Springs. It shut down when business dried up, but these days, thanks to Sally, it's back and better than ever!

It's carved right into the rock!

WILLY'S BUTTE

I got my first lesson in racing from Doc here on the dirt track at Willy's Butte. I still love to come up here and practice.

Watch out for that turn—it's tricky.

Watch out for those cacti—they're prickly.

FRANK'S FIELD

Mater is a master of the timeless art of tractor-tipping.

Mater always says:
Tractors is so dumb!

Oh, no! It's Frank!

THE FIRE STATION

Red the fire truck lives here in the fire station. He's been trying to get Bessie the road paver clean since 1967.

Fillmore's Organic Fuel

Fillmore is a good-hearted guy, and he sells some great organic fuel.

Farm-style windmill

Muffler wind-chime gate

Fillmore's dome

Oil-drum windmill

Night-vision goggles

Bedrolls

SARGE'S SURPLUS HUT

Sarge is Fillmore's neighbor. The two of them couldn't be more different . . . but they still get along pretty well.

THE NEW RACETRACK

After I finally made it to Los Angeles for the tiebreaking race, I decided it was time to find somewhere to call home. And what better place than Radiator Springs? Once I returned I started work on a new racetrack. It looks pretty cool, don't you think?

Grandstands

Lake

Press boxes

Pit

Main track

Home, sweet home ⟹

THE WINDING ROAD

Well, Mack and I have worn out a few sets of tires driving around this country. There's a lot to see and do out there, but Radiator Springs is the only place where I've ever wanted to get in a low gear and settle down. It has good scenery, great friends, and—oh, yes—the finest tractor-tipping this side of the Mississippi!